# 1

# YEAH, G'DAY.

It's me... the Narrator.

I've got another story for you.

We're back on Ithaca. It's been a long, hot summer. Our three Ithacan heroes – Nico, Claudia and Mikey – are enjoying the best surf ever. Well, Nico and Claudia are. Mikey, after seven years of almost daily surfing, still can't manage to stand on a board for more than three seconds; he's even worse when the board is in the water.

But Mikey believes that if at first you don't succeed, keep trying. Whereas I don't. I think if you are that bad at something you should chuck it in – give away your wetsuit, chainsaw your board in two... and take up synchronised swimming.

That's what I did. I took up synchronised swimming with some Narrator friends of mine. At first it was fun. But eventually their constant chattering nearly drove me mad. Imagine eight Narrators rabbiting on endlessly about synchronised swimming.

'We stick our feet up in the air, we wobble them about, we do a half somersault and stick our right hands up. The crowd goes wild.'

But I was finally forced to give it up when my friends refused to let me bring along my pet piranha.

## BUT ENOUGH ABOUT MY PROBLEMS, THERE'S A STORY WAITING TO BE TOLD.

So where was I?

Nico is a very happy monkey-headed Ithacan. All summer he has been competing in surf competitions. Now he has made it through to the finals of the World Surf Championships. Standing between Nico and the Champion's Cup is one person, Hercules, an overweight, lead-brained, has-been former champion with two left feet.

Nico is a certainty.

Nothing will keep him from the World Surf Championships, only four days away.

## NOTHING, THAT IS, UNTIL...

Nico is now faced with a very difficult decision. It is only four days till the World Surf Championships. Nico knows he can win. (Whereas I don't think he has a chance – he's got a head like a monkey!) So now his friends want him to take a long trip to Duryllium, maybe to find his friend Icon...who might be facing imprisonment, torture or even death.

Does he go? Or does he stay home and risk the anger of his friends, but maybe win the World Surf Champs? If he wins, it will be because of the tricks that very same Icon has taught him. That poor unfortunate Icon who could at this very moment be facing imprisonment, torture and death. So a hard choice! Save your friend or **BE WORLD SURF CHAMPION**. What would you do?

Staying home and watching TV is not an option.

Sending your little sister across the universe to do battle with a dangerous and deadly enemy while you stay home and watch TV is not an option either. Tough one, eh?

**GLORY OR LOYALTY.** What does he do?

Nico has made his choice. He will stay home and compete in the Champs. Do his friends support his decision? Of course they do.

'Well, we're off, you banana-breathed, low-down Judas, monkey-headed, ratbag son of a gorilla,' says Claudia.

'Oh, OK, cheerio then,' says Nico.

'Wish us luck,' says Claudia.

She shakes Nico's hand.

'So long, suckers. I'll show you my trophy when you get back.'

But Claudia does not let go of Nico's hand. She grips it even tighter. She and Mikey hold the M.I.T. and order it to take them to Icon.

'Noooooo! Let go of my hand, you…'

# PLIK!

Nico, Claudia and Mikey stand in a forest somewhere on Duryllium.

'The Championship! It was mine this year. I was a certainty. So where am I now? On some stupid planet in some stupid parallel universe looking for some bloke who is probably at home with his feet up watching TV. I should be home practising.'

Nico is not happy.

IT'S ONLY FOR A FEW DAYS, GRUMPY. YOU'LL STILL GET BACK IN TIME FOR YOUR STUPID SURF CHAMPIONSHIPS.

HUMPHH

SO WHERE IS ICON? HE MUST BE AROUND HERE SOME PLACE.

1001

Icon lies injured on the ground. All around him is the smoking wreckage and chaos of a battlefield. But the battle has moved on.

Meanwhile, lurking in the shadows near
the battlefield, King Vidor, Icon's misguided
brother, and Crundor, Vidor's loyal captain,
watch as Icon is carried away.

# 3

Vidor seems very pleased with himself. Which makes me ask, what is he up to? Did he set Icon up? In Duryllium, it is not acceptable to kill people unless it's absolutely necessary. And certainly it's not polite to kill princes. It's even worse manners to kill your brother...

And what is that around Vidor's neck?

My eyesight is hopeless since my little accident in Mecho-Africa on Other Earth 596 – a parallel universe I happened into by mistake one day when I went to buy the newspaper.

I was standing at what I thought was a grey coin-in-the-slot newspaper stand in the middle of a grassy plain. I was buying the *Nightly Bugle*, a very fine newspaper, and having a bit of trouble sticking the coin in the slot. 'Strange shaped slot,' I thought to myself. Suddenly...

# WHAM!

I felt like someone had thrown a piano at me. In fact it was a big Mecho-African rhinoceros. Hit me at 100 km per hour. From a standing start.

Anyway, my eyesight has never been the same. And I didn't get my coin back.

## BUT ENOUGH ABOUT MY PROBLEMS!

What is that around Vidor's neck? Not sure. But it looks like an eye to me. And where did he get it? Well, maybe that is why he is so pleased with himself. Maybe he took it from Icon.

But Icon has one around his neck, too. Hmmmm! Now I'm confused.

And I'm the Narrator!

# 4

Deep in the forest, there is a clearing. In the clearing there is a house. In the house there is a...

This sounds a bit like a lateral-thinking puzzle I once knew. In the house, there is a dead dwarf beside an unopened package, surrounded by a pool of water and two dying goldfish, and a surgeon whose son is on the operating table.

But this is not a lateral-thinking puzzle. I am trying to tell you where they are right now. And you are trying to sidetrack me. Well, pay attention, you reader thing, you.

Nico, Claudia and Mikey are walking up to this house, carrying Icon. They get to the front door. That's when they realise it is a Gingerbread House. They've never been in a Gingerbread House before. Claudia knocks on the door. What else is she going to do? They need help for Icon. And there isn't a house for miles (1.6 kms) around.

So she knocks.

## KNOCK KNOCK!!

Claudia has a very loud knock.

The cottage is very old and very messy.
And very small. In fact, there is not enough
room to swing a cat. Unless it is a very small
cat. Or a mouse. In fact, there's only just
enough room to swing a mouse.

They place Icon on a couch near the fire.
Delicious smells waft from a large cooking pot
bubbling away in the hearth – the sort of large
cooking pot that a witch, who lives in a
gingerbread cottage in the middle of a forest,
would use to cook up some children she has
captured. Once she has fattened them up, of
course. (Or was that an oven?)

It doesn't matter. She's not a witch! And
it's not children cooking in the pot. It's stew.
And the old woman ladles some out for
everyone. Then she cleans Icon's wound and
bandages his head.

YOUR FRIEND IS
BADLY WOUNDED.
WE WILL NEED
TO NURSE HIM
63 HOURS A
DAY.

HOW CAN WE
EVER THANK
YOU... ERH... UM.
WHAT DO WE
CALL YOU,
OLD WOMAN?

OLD
WOMAN.
THAT IS WHAT
MY FRIENDS
CALL ME.

SMALL
CAT

## 5

For four days, Icon lies on the couch in front of the fire. He lapses in and out of consciousness – a bit like a footballer on an end-of-season trip – sometimes muttering, sometimes screaming, sometimes shaking with fear, tormented by strange visions.

Days pass, or maybe weeks. It's hard to tell when you are in a Gingerbread House in the middle of a forest. But Nico has been cooped up for too long. He's slowly going mad. Not that anyone notices.

# 6

Now, I suppose you're wondering what King
Vidor is up to. Well, since we last called on
him, he has changed his hair colour five
times. Which you would know if you had the
colour version of this book. But all of those
were packed off to Planet Omega 13, where
everyone has more money than they know
what to do with.

They can afford colour copies of this book.
They can afford anything they want. They all
fly to school in stretch limos with spas and
twin tellies. They wash in baths full of warm
yoghurt. They don't have to eat cooked
cauliflower and white sauce. They have
someone who eats it for them.

Anyway, you have a black and white copy
of the book. That's just the way it is. Some
people are richer than others. Get used to it.
And you need to know that Vidor has
changed his hair colour.

He also has his army racing all over
Duryllium, disarming Icon's rebel forces. And
then, to teach them a lesson, he's burned

their villages. And their schools. And hospitals. And anything else that burns, including their dogs and cats, and birds and goldfish. But he doesn't harm the people, because it is not polite to kill people on Duryllium.

Then he rests. In fact, he spends a lot of time lying on the couch, polishing his Eye. The one hanging around his neck, that is. And while Vidor is polishing it, he imagines what a wonderful King he will make. And how grateful the people will be. Eventually.

One day, Vidor is sitting on the couch with Crundor, polishing his Eye very hard, when a puff of smoke blows up and they both disappear.

'What have you done, Vidor?' says Crundor.

'I was just rubbing my Eye.'

'I didn't know it could do that. What else is that Eye capable of?' says Crundor.

They look around. They are still sitting on the couch, but now they are perched at the top of a rocky outcrop. They are looking down on the city of Duryllium, which is also the capital of Duryllium.

'After the Contest, all of this will be mine, Crundor,' says Vidor.

'Ours, you mean!' thinks Crundor.

'I will be the True King of Duryllium and Icon will be destroyed. The people will come to love me. I will rule for fifty years. I will be the greatest King Duryllium has ever had. My father would be so proud of me, if he were alive.'

'Which he isn't,' adds Crundor.

'That was an unfortunate accident, Crundor. But he was old and his time had come. It was for the good of Duryllium. All of this is for the good of Duryllium,' says Vidor.

Vidor and Crundor stay on top of the mountain for some time, plotting the future of their Duryllium. Eventually they decide to return to the palace, which they manage to do fairly successfully. (Although a very old couple, making out in the park, have heart attacks when a large couch with the King on board hovers overhead.)

Back in the palace, Vidor announces:

'I think it is time we threw a big party, Crundor. And if we are lucky, Prince Icon might gatecrash it.'

## 7

Meanwhile, in a Gingerbread House in the middle of a clearing in a forest, an old woman talks to a young blind prince.

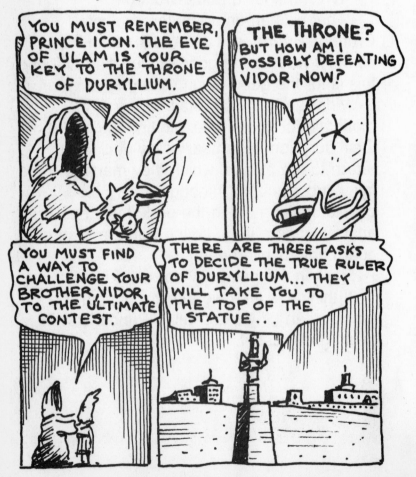

# 8

A large crowd has gathered outside the Royal Palace in Duryllium. Vidor stands on a small balcony, built for just a time as this – so that a King can stand above his people and talk down to them. Heads of Government always want to be higher than their people.

The crowd is watching Vidor very closely. Some Durylliumites want to hear him talk. But not many. Some want to see what their new King looks like. Again, not a lot. Most have come to admire his new hair colour, having read about it in the popular fashion magazine, *No Idea*.

And a precious few are throwing rocks and lumps of concrete and any parking inspectors they can find. They are angry with Vidor and with the chaos he has caused.

Vidor rests on the balcony rail, ignoring the parking inspectors wedged between the posts. He is telling the crowd of his great victory over the evil rebels, led by Icon.

You may feel a bit cheated, because I haven't given you Vidor's speech in full. But, believe me, you're lucky. Have you ever heard a King's speech in full? They do go on a bit. In fact, half the crowd start to clean their fingernails or remove lint from their pockets. The rest look around for a burger stand or simply fall asleep.

Then Vidor holds up the Eye. He tells the crowd that it is the Eye of Ulam, which makes him the True King of Duryllium. That wakes up some of the crowd. He then does a bit of the 'peace to all men' and 'long live Duryllium' kind of stuff. But most of the crowd don't take any notice. Even Crundor is starting to nod off.

But two members of the audience are very interested in the Eye.

'So, Vidor thinks he has the True Eye, does he?' says the tall woman, leaving quickly with her friend, a shorter, rounder man with a horn for a nose.

## 9

The Eyes have been used by the noble Kings and Queens of Duryllium throughout the centuries to help them rule wisely. But, during the rule of Queen Diana, the True Eye was lost. No one really knows how.

Every now and then, the Eye was found. The finder would claim to be the True One and would challenge the Ruler of Duryllium to the Eye Test. This Eye Test was not just a matter of looking at a chart and reading tiny letters.

It was a supreme test of leadership, involving three challenges of mind and body.

Because the Ruler might be old and not exactly physically fit, they could select a Second to do the challenge for them. The Second would usually be someone young and fit and smart. This meant the Ruler didn't even have to turn up. They could stay home with the dogs and watch it all on TV.

So, when a challenger fronted up for the test, they often found their opponent was a huge, super-fit genius. But the challenger wouldn't worry – the True Eye of Ulam would make them invincible.

After the First Challenge, they'd change their minds, of course, while plunging from a great height towards the ground. Not that they'd die. That is not the Duryllium way. Instead, they'd be imprisoned in the Underworld for the rest of their lives, or for eternity – whichever came first. Lucky break…except that they would be given some rotten job, like rolling a great ball of cow dung, the size of a piano, up a hill. And every time they'd get it to the top, the ball would roll back down the other side. So they would have to roll it up again. And again. And again. And again. Forever.

I've had worse jobs.

But this raises a problem for everyone gathered in the Gingerbread House. Who has the True Eye of Ulam? Vidor or Icon?

Has Vidor been given an Eye that he believes is the True Eye, but is really a False Eye...stolen by one of his agents from under the belly of a tired, old dragon in some far-off part of the Kingdom?

Or maybe, on the battlefield that day, Vidor switched Icon's True Eye for a False Eye. Which means that Vidor has the True Eye and Icon has the False Eye. But Icon still thinks he has the True Eye.

Now I'm getting a bit confused.

There is another possibility. Icon has the True Eye, but thinks it is a False Eye, because Vidor claims to have the True Eye (which is really false.)

And then there's another possibility. Icon has the True Eye. But Vidor thinks the Eye he has is the True one. But Vidor is quite happy to let Icon think Vidor's Eye might be the False Eye, so that Icon will challenge him, thinking that with the True Eye of Ulam he can't lose. When, really, he will. Lose, that is. Or...? Frankly, I can't remember who has the real Eye. And I'm starting to get a headache.

The important thing to know is that there is no way of telling whether you have the True Eye or the False one. Not until you undertake the Supreme Challenge. And there you are, up on the statue of Ulam the Magnificent, trying to fit the Eye into his eye socket. If it is the False Eye, next thing you know...

# PPPTTTUUUꜱꜱꜱ!!!

...it will be spat out, and you will be spat out with it, all the way to the Underworld, for eternity, or longer – rolling big balls of manure up hills. That's the breaks.

But there must be another way of telling whether it is True or False, I hear you ask. Perhaps there is a tiny, invisible-to-the-naked-eye symbol put there by the craftsman who carved it in the steamy sweatshops of the Underworld under the gaze of Nike, the Goddess of Eyeball-Carving.

No, sorry. There is no other way of telling. So, there.

On with the story!

37

38

# 10

We now move to the Royal Palace. A large crowd has gathered. But this time they are not throwing things, Vidor is! Tonight he is throwing a Masked Ball to celebrate his victory over Icon and the rebels.

All the rich and famous people of Duryllium are there in their finest clothes. The crowd is playing spot-the-celebrity. But it is a bit hard to know who's who because everyone is wearing a mask...after all, it is a Masked Ball.

There is the beautiful three-headed Martian opera singer, La Stupenda, with three sparkling new hairdos. There is the very rich media mogul from Zanadu, invisible in the costume of a chameleon. And the crowd cheers 'the Artist formally known as Elvis'. Even an elaborate costume and mask won't hide someone who weighs 300 kilograms and reeks of deep-fried peanut-butter.

Inside the Ballroom, a four-piece banjo band plays the same tune over and over again. This drives visitors from other planets mad. But the Durylliumites love it. It is the only tune they know.

This is because the Durylliumites are perfectly normal in every way, except for one peculiar thing. They have very poor musical memories.

They can remember smells forever. But smells are like that. We Narrators are very good with smells, too. And some smells are really worth remembering. Smells like bread baking in a small country town on a cold misty morning, while smoke wisps out of chimneys. Or old nappies! Old socks! Onions cooking! Smells carry lots of information and memories. Some of which you would rather forget. Like the smell of long-lost food deep down in your school bag. A dead rat under the fridge. Your best friend's farts.

The people of Duryllium are able to smell something today and tell you when and where they last smelt it, who was there at the time, what they were wearing and even whether they had their shoelaces tied with single or double knots. (And, by the way, double knots are always safer.) And they can tell you this even if it was ten years ago. Or twenty.

But play them a song and ask them to hum a few bars from memory and they will look at you blankly, saying: 'What song?'

Songs go in one ear and out the other.

Which is not a bad thing if you think about it.

Because Durylliumites can't keep a tune in their heads for more than five seconds, rather than produce a whole lot of songs no one would remember, they have only ever produced one song. Luckily, everybody loved it. (Not that they remembered it.)

So, tonight the band is playing that one song over and over and over again. And there is a tall woman, in an elephant-head mask, who is slowly going mad. She is about to go ballistic and dismantle the lead banjo player.

Standing next to her is someone who looks like a walking post-box. He is dressed up as an obscure, Southern Hemisphere, Earth outlaw called Ned Kelly. He was a man who took to wandering around in a suit of armour made of steel, taking other people's things because he was too poor to have any things of his own. But that's another story. This Ned Kelly also had a helmet made of steel. Nico has a helmet, but it is not steel. It is made of recycled pig saliva, or something like that. I can't remember and it doesn't matter. What does matter is that he is getting a little annoyed because people keep posting things in his eye-slot. Standing next to him is a large tree, with a horn.

King Vidor, splendidly dressed as a duck, welcomes all the masked Durylliumites. Beside him stands a grumpy, maskless Crundor. He hates all parties.

Later in the night, the tall elephant-headed woman, who claims to be Ganesha, lures Duck Man Vidor out onto the balcony. She piles on the charm and keeps him talking. Vidor blathers on about being King…and how the people adore him…blah, blah, blah…and how he has the Eye of Ulam…blah, blah, blah…and how he is going to challenge his brother…and how his brother couldn't possibly win…

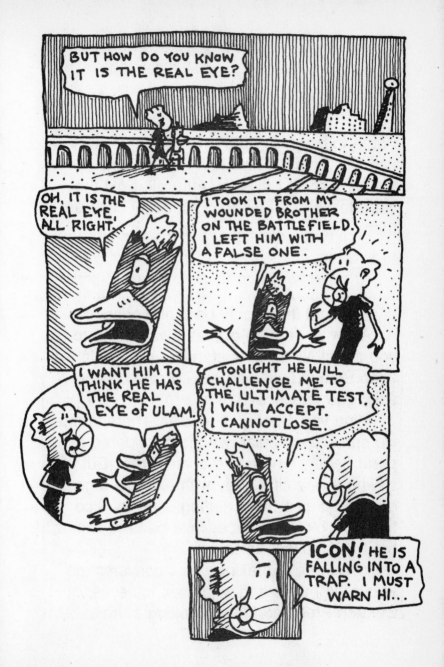

45

# 11

I hate to break in here and interrupt…well, actually, I don't. I love it. If I didn't, you wouldn't know I existed. After all, I **AM** the Narrator. And if I were to suddenly clam up then.....................................................................
..............................................................................
..............................................................................
.......................
..............and that would be a bit boring.

Anyway, enough of that. I was going to tell you about Nico. He is standing on the dance floor. Beautiful women are coming up and asking to dance with him.

Mind you, beauty is relative. There is one woman, in particular, who is considered a great beauty where she comes from. But having a beautiful body with external digestive organs takes a bit of getting used to. Nico tries to look at her face while he talks to her, but his mind wanders.

While she is making polite conversation about the music and whatever, his eyes wander. Pretty soon he's looking at her pulsating external brain, then he is focusing on her see-through stomachs and intestines …watching the avocados she has just eaten turn into guacamole. She eventually gives up and leaves him alone.

He's a one-girl man, our Nico. And that one girl is outside on the balcony with Vidor. And, besides, Nico is miles away. He's dreaming of the World Surf Championships. And through the miracle of modern publishing we can bring you that dream.

# OK!

Back to the Palace Ballroom. Claudia, masquerading as Ganesha, is desperate to warn Icon that he is falling into a trap. But it is too late.

Suddenly, there is a lot of murmuring as the crowd of masked revellers part. Someone steps through the gap. Every mask turns to look. It is someone short, dressed in a costume that makes them look like the spitting image of Prince Icon.

No. Wait. It **IS** Prince Icon. And without a mask. How did he get in without a mask? But don't worry about that – it isn't important. What is important is what happens next.

49

50

51

# 13

(Don't read this chapter, it is bad luck.)

Icon walks up the gangway of a large ocean liner about to depart on its maiden voyage. Icon is escaping his responsibilities again. It is April 14, 1912. Planet Earth. The ship is called *Titanic*. Now, that's bad luck!

It sails off into a clear night. Not an iceberg to be seen. That's good luck!

But suddenly the ship hits a huge iceberg. An invisible iceberg. That's bad luck!

Invisible icebergs? This must be a parallel universe, where things are almost the same but different. In fact, the *Titanic* keeps sailing. Not a hole in her. That's good luck!

But now the invisible iceberg begins to sink. And thousands of invisible penguins start to sink with it. They jump into the water. But, as you know, invisible penguins can't swim. So, all night long, the silent cries of invisible penguins drowning are heard by no one. That's bad luck!

The *Titanic* arrives safely at its destination. Icon leaves the ship. He wanders off into the big city to start a new life. Our story ends. Now, that's bad luck!

Or is it? (I warned you not to read this chapter.)

# 14

This is not going well for Icon and the Ithacans. And Claudia knows it. She must get away from Vidor and find Nico and Mikey.

'I must powder my nose, your Vidorship,' she says, and heads off through the crowd.

This makes no sense to Vidor. Powder your nose? People on Duryllium take things very literally. Vidor's mind fills with visions of his new friend Ganesha grinding her nose to powder. But he loves her large trunky nose. He is upset. He tries to imagine her face with no nose. This is too much.

Then, he thinks, what does she do with the powder? It suddenly hits him. She loves him so much that at this very moment she is standing with her nose to the grindstone, turning her nose into powder so she can give it to him as a token of her undying love for him.

Vidor stands on the balcony, a broad smile sweeping across his face. Ganesha loves Vidor. He takes out his Duryllium hunting knife and spends the rest of the night carving that in the balustrade.

Ganesha Loves Vidor. Ganesha Loves Vidor. Ganesha Loves Vidor. Ganesha Loves Vidor. Twenty-three times.

55

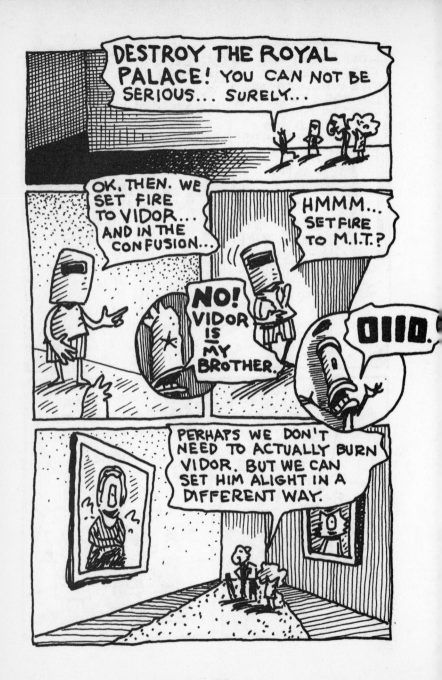

# 15

Now I have some bad news for you. There is

# NO
# CHAPTER
# 15.

Sorry!

# 15

(Please ignore previous Chapter 15.)

Later that night, back in Vidor's private suite, the lovers talk. If you are not into mushy love scenes you could skip this chapter. But if you do choose to skip this chapter…

## BE WARNED!

…you will lose track of the story and end up horribly confused. And you will miss a lot of lovely kissing!

Personally, I love kissing. I can't get enough of it. I kiss Mrs Narrator at least twenty times a day. And, if she is not around, I kiss her photo instead. In fact, I often have to go down to the print shop and get a new 10x8 of her, because I've worn out the old one. Mrs Narrator is not around much at the moment. I think she has left home.

It's because of the kissing, a bit. But it's more because of my breath. You see, I love garlic. Can't get enough of it. It wards off the vampires. And there are a lot of those around where I live. And you have to eat garlic to be sure. Vampires hate garlic. So do a lot of other things, too. Mosquitoes hate it.

And do we have big mosquitoes here. So big, you can hear them coming for kilometres. So big, they will carry off your dog. There was one so big the other day that they had to call out the army, which eventually knocked it out of the air with a surface-to-air missile. But that's another story!

# BACK TO THE BEDROOM!

Vidor is trying to get Claudia to take off her mask so he can set his beady eyes on his future Queen.

'No, my little duckling,' she says, 'let's have some more champagne.'

You don't have to ask that little black duck twice. He adores champagne. Perhaps a little too much for his own good.

They walk out onto the balcony. Vidor snuggles up very close to Claudia. She thinks about clobbering him, but resists for the moment. Vidor rabbits on about the Contest …and becoming the True Ruler of Duryllium …and destroying Icon…and much more.

But Claudia keeps feeding him champagne. And every time Vidor stops talking, she raises her glass and they drink to whatever it was he was saying. Vidor drinks, but Claudia doesn't. She tips hers out over the edge of the balcony.

Two guards, Derek and Gordon, are on duty below the balcony. They are starting to get wet.

'Looks like rain, Derek,' says Gordon.

'Where?' says Derek.

'Up there,' says Gordon.

And, like a fool, Derek looks up, only to get an eye-full of Claudia's champagne.

Gordon is now standing quite happily under his little mini umbrella. Smiling.

'Where did you get that…? GRRRR!' Derek is not happy.

On the balcony above, Vidor is a little all over the place. He is now looking at Claudia. Which is difficult because the champagne is making him see about three Claudias. He is focusing on the one in the middle and telling her what a wonderful Queen she would make, for the one thousandth time. Then he makes a big mistake. He tries to plant a kiss on her elephant cheek, he tries to caress her trunk.

She knocks him out. Not that he notices really, because he was halfway there already.

Then she drags him to his bed.

# 16

Meanwhile, on a far-off planet in a parallel universe, the astronomer Pterodactyl ponders a problem, as his world turns upside-down.

# 16 (again)

Nico is dreaming about the World Surf Championships. He is on the final wave. And it's a whopper. Hercules, Nico's arch-rival, is on the wave, too. It's a head-to-head, first-one-to-wipe-out-loses, winner-takes-all surf-off. Nico is hot. He does a Frontside Air, then a Layback Snap with Pike, then finishes off with a mind-blowing Forehand Snap and a nice Hip-Pocket and two Tucks with Pleat to Mid-Calf Length. Very fashionable.

But he nails it. And Hercules, desperate to beat Nico, flies straight up the face of the same wave, attempts a Frontside Air and junks out. Well, actually, he crashes into a No Boating sign.

The crowd roars.

'Nico! Nico! Nico!'

'Nico! Nico, come on.' It is Mikey.

Worse, this has all been a dream. No World Championship for Nico.

'We've got to meet Claudia! Come on.'

They take hold of the M.I.T. and, thinking of Claudia… **PLIK!**

# PLIK!

They miss. They are standing in a small
open space with stone
walls all around. The
walls are very high and
very smooth. On one
wall there are two carved
symbols. Nico
and Mikey take a long
look at them. One is

definitely a stick figure person. The other one,
they don't recognise. But it looks as if it might
mean 'Release the Hounds!'

'Any ideas?' says Nico.

'Yes, one. Let's get out of here,' says Mikey.

They grab hold of the M.I.T.

'Take us to Claudia,' they say.

But nothing happens.

'**101101!**' screams the M.I.T.

They try another half a dozen times. Zilch!

Then Mikey has a brilliant thought.

'We must be in the Underworld,' he says.

'Mikey! The walls are moving.'

And, sure enough, the space is much smaller than when they first arrived. And getting smaller. The symbols on the wall seem to be their only hope. But which one? They pick the stick figure.

# BOING!!!

68

69

# 17

The morning after the Ball, King Vidor awakens from dreams of glory. Today is his big day. The prize, for which he has been preparing all his life, is about to be handed to him. And poor Icon has no hope. He just doesn't know it. By tonight, Vidor will be King of Duryllium once and for all. And his beautiful Ganesha will be his Queen. If only he can find her and ask her to marry him.

After applying make-up to hide his black eye, he rushes downstairs. No one has seen his beautiful Ganesha since she fled the palace around midnight. His elephant princess is gone.

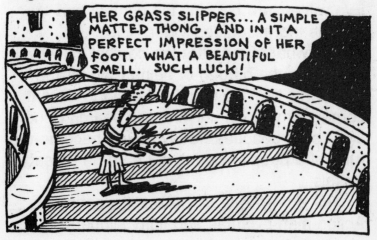

HER GRASS SLIPPER... A SIMPLE MATTED THONG. AND IN IT A PERFECT IMPRESSION OF HER FOOT. WHAT A BEAUTIFUL SMELL. SUCH LUCK!

# **17** (Part 2)

It is nearly dawn.

Icon gazes out over the city of Duryllium. Well, he would if his eyes were working. Today is a big day. In his hands he holds the Eye of Ulam and the fate of his people. This is a big burden for one man. Icon believes the Eye will ensure he wins the contest and defeats the misguided Vidor.

But what about after the contest? How will he handle the burden of being King for the rest of his life? No more escaping to distant corners of various universes in search of new and better beaches. Today he will become the ruler of a people. Icon is not sure he is ready for this.

Nor am I! After all, he is still wearing his Action-man pyjamas and fluffy slippers.

The people of Duryllium are gathered around a platform at the base of the statue of Ulam the Magnificent. They are here to witness a contest between the two rivals for the throne of Duryllium. The winner will be the One True Ruler of all Duryllium. The loser…well, where I come from, the loser would sell his story and soul to the media and become a celebrity millionaire, spending the rest of his days appearing on chat shows and charity night panels. Anyway, I don't care about losers. It's winners I want. And lots of them.

But in this contest there can be only ONE winner. And I know who it is. But I'm not telling. Quiet! The announcer is introducing the contestants.

Why the statue of Ulam the Magnificent? Good question. Ulam the Magnificent was a great and legendary leader of Duryllium in the Days of Yore, before the Age of Uncertainty. His statue carries the Three Talents of Leadership. The Sword of Strength, the Book of Knowledge and the Eye of Vision. Actually, there was a fourth, the Finger of Fate. But that fell off. Nobody ever really understood what it meant, so they didn't bother to replace it. It eventually turned up on Planet Earth in the British Museum.

Then the Eye disappeared in the Age of Uncertainty. No one knows who took it.

There was a rumour I heard that an old tourist from Canis Minor was visiting the area after the Great Earthquake of '42. Near the statue, he found an interesting round white rock half buried in the sand. He was a rock collector. And this was a beauty. So he took it back home to Canis Minor and popped it up on his mantelpiece. He didn't give it another thought.

After he died, it was sold to a travelling pedlar, who sold it to an old man who sold it to a young woman who sold it to an older man…and, next thing we know, it turns up stuck in the eye socket of a huge statue of a chicken in a maze in the Duryllium Underworld.

# BUT THAT'S ANOTHER STORY.

Back to the Contest! The third and final test is to climb the statue and place the Eye in the empty eye socket of Ulam the Magnificent. Only the bearer of the True Eye will succeed. Although having the True Eye doesn't necessarily mean you will succeed, as Gondor the Great found out several centuries ago. He climbed all the way to the top with the Eye. He nearly fell many times, but he did get to the top. Though, in the process, he lost his glasses. Without them, he was blind as a Venutian Vampire Bat…and I'm sure I don't have to tell you how blind they are. (Which is lucky, because I don't know.)

So, anyway, he couldn't see where he was putting the Eye. He stuffed it up Ulam's nose. The statue rumbled and grumbled and eventually sneezed the Eye clear across Duryllium. Gondor, who was still holding onto the Eye, went with it, never to be seen again. Ulam's nose went with him, too. And that has never been seen again either.

EACH CONTESTANT IS ALLOWED A SECOND. HAVE YOU MADE YOUR CHOICE?

I HAVE CHOSEN AS MY SECOND, CAPTAIN CRUNDOR!

## 19

The beginning of this Supreme Contest is not as exciting as it should be. Especially if you are part of the crowd and you have paid good money to come along to see a bit of biffo. Supreme Contests are not like that.

The two teams start on opposite sides of the huge statue of Ulam the Magnificent, the length of a football field apart. There is no running. No chest beating. No grunting. They are just looking at what lies before them, knowing that one wrong move could kill them. And they know to expect the unexpected.

Before them is a moat. No water. Just a sandy floor. There must be some danger here, because these are the Pits of Doom. In the Pits of Doom, they are not going to meet fluffy dogs and fairy floss. Unless they are vicious neck-ripping fluffy dogs and napalm fairy floss.

ARGHHH! WE'RE GOING TO DIE... RIPPED TO PIECES BY BLOOD-THIRSTY BONECRUNCHERS! OH, WOE IS ME. SO FAR FROM HOME, NOW I'LL NEVER BECOME WORLD SURF CHAMPION!!

NICO, WOULD YOU HAND ME THE BACK PACK.

WHAT? WHY?

I WAS EXPECTING THIS. MY BACK PACK... THERE IS A METAL CANISTER.

GET IT OUT AND I SUGGEST YOU HURRY.

UM... ERR... METAL CANISTER, IN HERE SOMEWHERE.

# 20

The crowd is silent. They can't see a thing.
The two teams are below the ground and out
of sight. The crowd has no idea what is going
on. As far as they know, the contestants could
be sitting together having a cup of tea and
discussing the weather. The crowd is getting
restless.

Those who support Vidor are wearing
blue and white. Icon's supporters are in red.
The two groups of supporters are starting to
pick fights with each other. Someone in blue
pours his drink over someone in red, who
throws his can at someone in blue, who
chucks a chair at someone in red, who biffs
someone else on the nose. A flare is lit and
thrown into a group of drunken blue
boys… **AND THEN ALL HELL
BREAKS LOOSE.**
The crowd is happily rioting, when a distant
figure climbs out of the Pits of Doom. The
crowd goes silent. With hands around choking
necks, heads gripped in headlocks and chests
being sat on, they all stop…and look.

First Vidor and Crundor emerge. There is warm applause. Then the crowd waits. And waits. Then Icon and Nico climb out.

# THE CROWD GOES WILD.

Everybody loves the underdogs.

# 21

With the Pits of Doom behind them, the
contestants – still on opposite sides of the
giant statue – move on to the next test.
Before them is an open space paved with a
stone mosaic. Harmless enough, you might
think. But here there is only one true path. If
you are careful you will walk across solid
stones to glory. If you are foolish and take the
wrong path, you might plunge into the Depths
of Gloom, or step on an exploding stone,
scattering your body to the four winds.

It is a bit like walking through my house in
the dark…in bare feet. One false move and
you might step on a plastic toy, a Screaming
Doll, or a Plutonian Pussy Cat. Or, as you are
about to step into bed, your foot might
manage to find your son's collection of rare
Abyssinian Stone Fish, which he has lovingly
assembled by your bedside. The sharp Stone
Fish rip through your flesh, depositing their
deadly poison in your foot. Less than three
minutes later, you are writhing and screaming
in the back of an ambulance, rushing off to
the emergency ward of the local hospital

where the doctors will spend the next few
hours deciding who will have the pleasure of
chopping off your foot. Or whether they should
take both feet off just to make things even.
I always walk around my house at night in
heavy military boots. And I stomp!

But back to the action.

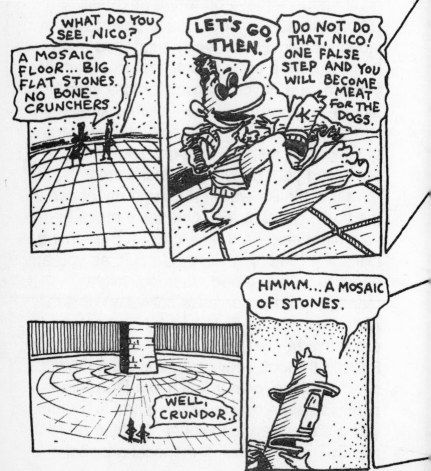

97

# 22

Slowly, ever so slowly, Icon and Nico crawl their way across the stone mosaic. Really slowly, extremely slowly. Till, eventually, they reach the foot of the giant statue.

The crowd stops its orgy of strangulation and walloping, briefly, to cheer on Icon and Nico. But these are muffled cheers. Cheers for a good try. Job well done. 'Good to see you made it through that test, but now we are stuck with Vidor for King for the rest of our lives' type cheers. And 'how come we supported a pathetic loser who has given us hope then failed to deliver' type cheers. Cheers-that-turn-into-tears type cheers.

And now Nico is suddenly thinking of last year's Surf Championships – the semi-finals, when he missed one vital wave and for the rest of the day was always one wave behind. Playing catch-up. He thinks that he and Icon are now in a similar position.

**WAKE UP, YOU MONKEY-BRAINED SON OF A CHIMPANZEE!!** There is no choice here. There is no way back, unless you want to tackle the mosaic again. You forgot to pack your jetpack. There are no emergency stairs. So the only way out is up. Forget about your problems and self doubts, **JUST GET ON WITH IT!**

Well, that's what I would tell Nico and Icon if I was their coach, and this was half-time in a game of Hand-Grenade Cricket, my favourite sporting pastime. But I'm not their coach. And they probably wouldn't listen anyway; no one ever listens to Narrators. Except you, of course.

And it's not quite true that there is no way of escaping. In fact, there is a large stone on the ground marked with a very small carved stick figure. But, after Nico's previous experience, there is no way he will touch this stone. Which is a pity really, because it opens a door to a stairway that leads all the way to the top of the statue. It's for the cleaners.

Nico is not looking at stones. He is looking up.

## 23

From the top of the Statue of Ulam, the view is magnificent. (That's a little joke!)

From the bottom it is all uphill.

It's all uphill from here. And hard work, too. Can you imagine what it is like to have to climb up a vertical wall with only a rope to hang on to? Dragging your own weight against the force of gravity. And if you're like me, that's a heck of a lot of weight. The pain as the muscles scream out:

# STOP! I CAN'T TAKE ANY MORE.

They just want rest. They just want you to let go. What do they care if you plunge twenty metres to a hard stone floor? They are just muscles. Dumb muscles.

# 24

The game is up. Vidor and Crundor have climbed to the top of the statue and stand there victorious. There is only one thing left to be done. What's that, you ask?

**HAVEN'T YOU BEEN LISTENING???**

Do you think they are up there to make daisy chains??

Actually, when I first read this story, that's exactly what I thought they were going to do. Sit there and make a few daisy chains. Pop them on their heads and sing a little skipping song, which would have been nice. But as my wife pointed out, where are they going to get the daisies from when they are on top of a huge stone statue? Good point, Mrs Narrator. There is never a daisy seller around when you want one. I suppose if they had their phones with them, they could call Dial-a-Daisy, for home delivery within half an hour. But they haven't got phones. They don't need daisies. They are not making daisy chains.

So, the crowd stands breathless as Vidor moves towards the Statue of Ulam, with the Eye.

# BIG MOMENT THIS!

If Vidor has the True Eye, it is the end for Icon. And makes a mess of the story, frankly. We all might as well go home. You can close the book and get some shut-eye.

But if Vidor doesn't have the True Eye... then, beauty, the story gets interesting. A happy ending is just around the corner.

# ARE YOU NERVOUS?

I know I am.

It's a bit like the Great Narrators' Bake-off of '56. There were three of us in the running. I had chosen to bake a pav. As I was mixing the egg-whites there was a sense of fear and trepidation. My Second was busily mopping my brow. I was bathed in a sea of sweat. I folded in the sugar very slowly, taking great care. Too slowly and the egg-whites might lose their fluff. Too quickly and the sugar won't dissolve. My nerves on the edge, I carefully poured the mixture onto the pre-greased tray. Into a moderate oven...but not too moderate. And then the long wait.

Nearly killed me. I've never known such tension.

When the timer went off and I pulled the

pav from the oven, **SUCH JOY!** The pav was a beauty. Tall, strong and so sugary white. My Second and I danced for joy. The faces of the other contestants sank into desperation.

Did I win? NO! Of course not. Something always goes wrong. At the height of our joy, I caught my foot in the hem of my apron. I knew I should have worn the short apron. I tripped forward, knocking over my Second, who stood on the cat, which leapt onto the table, knocking over the soy sauce, which detonated a box of party poppers. The shock waves caused my award-winning pav to collapse and sink flatter than…something that's really flat…and with it went my chances of becoming the Universe-wide Narrators' Bake-off Champion. Again.

So I understand nervous.

# 25

Meanwhile, on the ground, Nico cradles the semi-conscious Icon, who is rambling on and and on and on, and making no sense whatsoever. No sense to anyone but Nico, who is busily taking notes of everything Icon says.

'…sox bigger than a bread box I told the pink volcano, who was wearing my two-litre, five-speed octopus…'

Suddenly, Nico sees something plummeting from the top of the statue. Actually, it's two somethings.

It takes Nico a few seconds to process the information. An electric pulse travels from his eyes to his brain, but for a while it gets stuck on a big knob in the front of his brain. This is a knob of old chewing-gum that Nico has swallowed over the years. It all went to his brain. And that's not all that has ended up there. In a back corner are also two long-lost pieces of Lego and three odd blue socks that his mum has been looking for for years.

Anyway, to cut a short story long, the information eventually gets to the important parts of his brain. Nico recognises the plungers as Vidor and Crundor. And then he figures that their Eye must have been the False Eye...which is clever for Nico. So he figures that Icon is holding the True Eye.

Only problem is that Icon is on the ground raving like a drunk goat. But Nico now knows that they can win this contest, if only he can get Icon up to the top of the statue, somehow. Then he has another brainwave. Two in one day, that's a record!

# THE OLD ITHACAN ROPE TRICK.

When Nico was a boy, his old Uncle Nicodermis taught him how to throw a rope. They spent hours in the backyard lassoing things, usually the dog and the cat, but sometimes the chooks – they were harder because they were occasionally awake, which the dog and cat never were.

Eventually, Nico became an even better rope thrower than his Uncle Nicodermis. Which isn't saying much, because his uncle was hopeless.

So Nico throws his trusty rope and lassoes a part of the statue, at the very top...on his twenty-seventh attempt. Now they can haul themselves to the top, pop the Eye in place and return to the bottom heroes. Easy!

# 13x2

As Icon is placing the Eye into the statue of
Ulam the Magnificent, all of Duryllium holds
its breath.

Let's hope he doesn't take a week to do
the deed or everyone in Duryllium will die
from holding their breath and there will be a
huge pile of one-eyed bodies, and some lone
cleaner, who wasn't holding his breath at the
time, will have to clean up the mess.

Senior citizens, young babies,

even small dogs
hold their breath.

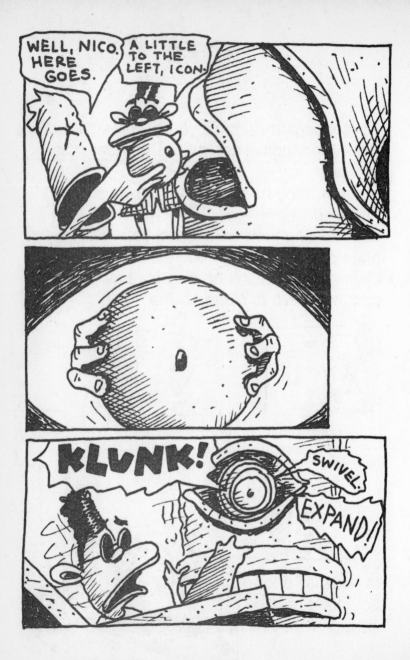

124

Happy ending! Now that's a lucky break.
It was the right Eye after all.

The  crowd goes berserk, again. And now Icon, or should I say **KING ICON**, introduces to the crowd those who have helped him in this quest: Claudia, the supreme manipulator; Mikey, the cunning planner; and Nico…well, what can we say about Nico? Icon's Second in the Supreme Contest! The one who, when all seemed lost, single-handedly dragged Icon up the face of the statue to meet with destiny. As the crowd roars, Icon grants the Ithacans the freedom of Duryllium.

'Anything you are wanting, it is yours,' cries King Icon.

'Anything?' says Mikey.

'That was a mistake,' says Claudia.

So what is Nico going to ask for? A week on a deserted tropical island with Claudia? Two weeks on a nudist deserted tropical island, with you know who? Three weeks? Actually, if he had thought about it, that's what he would have wished for. But his mind doesn't work as quickly as mine. We Narrators are very quick-witted.

'Anything?' says Nico.

'Anything,' says Icon.

'Well, there are the World Surf Championships!!!'

# 28

Meanwhile, deep down in the Pits of Doom, something stirs. Is it the Loch Ness Monster? The Zombie from the Dark Lagoon? A sewerage inspector? A backwards Mikey from the first story? Actually, that's a good idea! But it's too late for good ideas. It's…It's…

…two wretched figures, who climb out of the Pits of Doom and slink off into the dusky gloom.

So, there ends our tale. And magnificently narrated it was, too. Thank you! But I mustn't stick around, I've got another Bake-off. And there is no more story to tell.

Except to point out to you that a lonely, dejected figure is sitting on a beach somewhere on Ithaca. Unfortunately, he arrived back too late to compete in the World Surf Champs. But now he is thinking about all he has been through. He has travelled across the Universe. He has climbed mighty towers. He has almost single-handedly rescued a King and Country. Do you think he cares about some stupid Surf Championship?

## YOU BET HE DOES!!!

Nico is NOT happy.
Still, there's always next year.
He'll get over it.

# A GUIDE TO M.I.T.'S* LANGUAGE

| | |
|---|---|
| 1 | I hate surfing |
| 0 | There's lice in here! |
| 01 | You idiot! |
| 10 | I hate sand |
| 11 | Bummer |
| 010 | Hello, master |
| 011 | Goodnight |
| 101 | Pooh! |
| 110 | Ouch |
| 0000 | My yak has fleas! |
| 0100 | That's handy |
| 0010 | Oh, joy! |
| 0001 | HELP! |
| 0101 | You double idiot! |
| 0110 | Why me? |
| 1001 | ICON! |
| 1110 | Icon's in danger! |
| 00000 | My head hurts |
| 00110 | The roof is leaking |
| 10001 | Die, you fiend! |
| 11010 | I was right. A whole other world. What an ugly looking being. |
| 11011 | Smarter than you, lizard-brains! |
| 10111 | Panic stations!! |
| 11101 | What do you think I just said, blockhead? |
| 11110 | This way, boneheads! |
| 100011 | I want my mummy |
| 100101 | There's someone out there watching me! |
| 100111 | Quiet, you stupid animal-head people |
| 101010 | Put me down! |
| 101101 | I don't work in the underworld, idiot |
| 101110 | What the *&^%$# am I doing here? |
| 111000 | As it happens, I play with my feet |
| 111101 | The kettle's boiling |
| 111010 | I hate water! |
| 111001 | My feet are on fire |
| 1110111 | Yes! |

*M.I.T. (pronounced *em-eye-tee*) is short for Mental Image Transfer.